Disney
Peter Pan

*This is the story of Peter Pan—
the boy who never wanted to grow up!*

Long ago in London there lived three children—Wendy, John, and Michael.

Wendy told her brothers stories about a faraway place—Never Land. The hero of these stories was Peter Pan, a boy who *never* grew up, and who had wonderful adventures.

One night, when the children were fast asleep, Peter Pan and his friend, the fairy Tinker Bell, flew in through the nursery window. They had come to search for Peter's shadow. Peter had left it behind one night while he was listening to one of Wendy's stories.

Just then, Wendy woke up. She was thrilled to meet Peter Pan and agreed to help him and Tinker Bell capture the mischievous shadow.

Peter liked Wendy and urged her to fly with him to Never Land. "You *never* grow up there!" he promised.

Wendy agreed at once, as long as her brothers could come, too.

So, Peter told Wendy, John, and Michael to each think happy thoughts. Then he sprinkled them with magic pixie dust.

Before they knew it, the excited children were soaring high above the rooftops of London.

"Second star to the right and straight on till morning," Peter called, leading the way.

The children flew all the way to the enchanted world of Never Land—home to Peter and the Lost Boys, the dreaded Captain Hook, his ship of pirates, and mermaids!

While Peter was out with Wendy at the Mermaids'
Lagoon, Peter spotted a little rowboat in the distance.
"It's Hook, alright!" he cried.
Captain Hook was a wicked pirate and Peter Pan's
greatest enemy. Once, in a fierce battle, Peter had cut
off Hook's hand. The pirate now had a terrible steel
hook attached to his left wrist.

And where did that hand go?

A hungry crocodile had eaten the pirate's hand! He had enjoyed his meal so much that he now followed Hook everywhere, hoping for a chance to gobble up the rest of him!

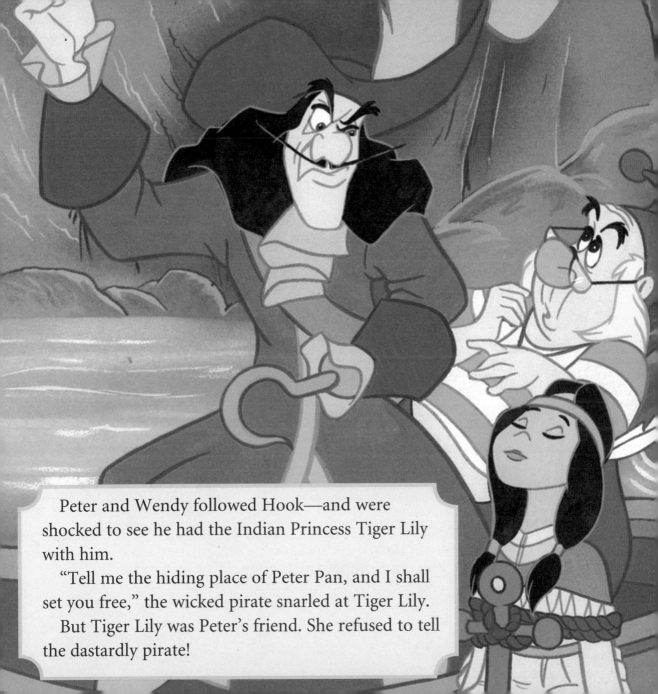

Peter and Wendy followed Hook—and were shocked to see he had the Indian Princess Tiger Lily with him.

"Tell me the hiding place of Peter Pan, and I shall set you free," the wicked pirate snarled at Tiger Lily.

But Tiger Lily was Peter's friend. She refused to tell the dastardly pirate!

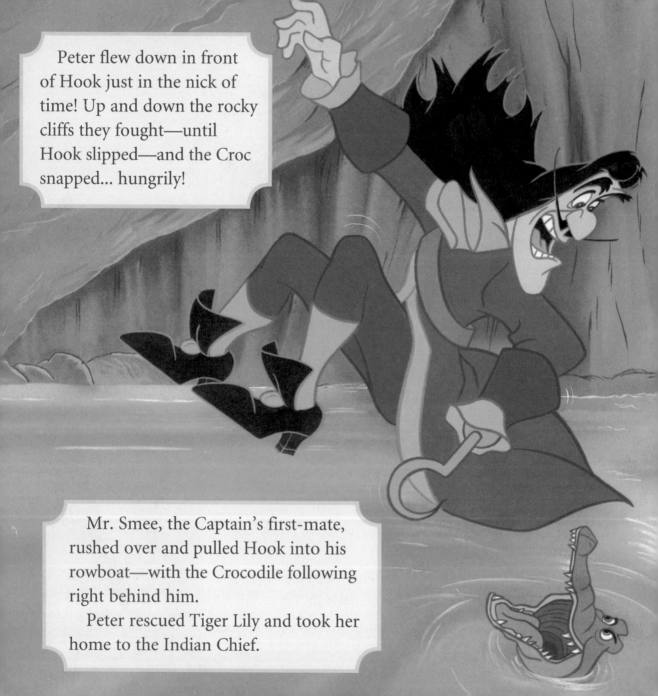

Peter flew down in front of Hook just in the nick of time! Up and down the rocky cliffs they fought—until Hook slipped—and the Croc snapped... hungrily!

Mr. Smee, the Captain's first-mate, rushed over and pulled Hook into his rowboat—with the Crocodile following right behind him.

Peter rescued Tiger Lily and took her home to the Indian Chief.

Back at Peter's hideout, Wendy told the boys their favorite story.

But they were all very homesick.

"I want my mother," sobbed Michael.

And although the Lost Boys didn't know what a mother was, they decided they wanted one, too.

So, Wendy promised that they would all go back to her London home together.

But Captain Hook and the other pirates were waiting outside the hideout. The pirates captured the children and took them back to Hook's ship!

Hook gave them a choice: Join the pirates or walk the plank!

The boys rather liked the idea of becoming pirates, but Wendy didn't.

"Peter Pan will save us!" she said.

Hook laughed loudly. "We left a present for Peter—a surprise package!" It was a bomb! "Peter Pan will be blasted out of Never Land *forever*!"

Tinker Bell overheard
these words. She knew she
had to warn Peter. The tiny
fairy reached Peter's hideout
just as he was about to open
the present.

She grabbed the bomb and threw it as far away as she could. Seconds later, there was one *huge* explosion.

Tinker Bell told Peter that Wendy and the others were in danger, and Peter sped off to rescue them with Tinker Bell close behind.

Peter Pan arrived just in time to save Wendy
and the boys! He turned to face his enemy.

Back and forth went Peter and Hook in the
most terrible battle ever fought.

Hook lunged at Peter, who fought back,
forcing the Captain to slip and fall backward…

...into the water below, where the hungry Crocodile waited.

The children clapped and cheered as they watched Hook frantically swimming toward Smee's rowboat, pursued by the snapping jaws of the Croc.

Peter gave the order to raise the anchor. Tinker Bell sprinkled the pirate ship with magic pixie dust, and in no time at all, the ship was soaring high above Never Land. It flew all the way to London, where Wendy, John, and Michael were soon safely back in their nursery.

As the children waved good-bye,
the pirate ship sailed off into the night sky,
silhouetted against the full moon…

...for Peter Pan, Tinker Bell, and the Lost Boys (who weren't *quite* ready to grow up yet) were off on another wonderful Never Land adventure.